Milo & the Monster

by David Michael Slater

illustrated by Jeff Ebbeler

magic
wagon

visit us at www.abdopublishing.com

For Rachel, Andy & their new monster—DMS

Text by David Michael Slater
Illustrations by Jeff Ebbeler
Edited by Stephanie Hedlund and Rochelle Baltzer
Interior layout and design by Becky Daum
Cover design by Becky Daum

Library of Congress Cataloging-in-Publication Data
Slater, David Michael.
  Milo & the monster / by David Michael Slater ; illustrated by Jeff Ebbeler.
     p. cm.
  Summary: Milo battles a monster while attempting to tell his story in the classroom book nook.
  ISBN 978-1-60270-656-9 (alk. paper)
  [1. Monsters--Fiction. 2. Books--Fiction. 3. Storytelling--Fiction. 4. Schools--Fiction.] I. Ebbeler, Jeffrey, ill. II. Title. III. Title: Milo and the monster.
  PZ7.S62898Mg 2009
  [E]--dc22
                                  2008055343

Hi, my name is Milo.
This is my story.

It all started when I kinda freaked out in the Book Nook. It was All About Me time during Sharing. I was next, so I grabbed the biggest book I could find and stuck my head in it.

No, I'm saying,
I stuck my head in it!

It was so quiet in there—
like my own secret world.

Hi my name is Milo.
This is my story.

Aren't you even gonna put up a fight? You could at least make the last thing you do interesting.

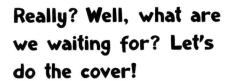

Why? No one will even care if I get eaten in this story. I bet they'll love you though. Everybody loves stories about monsters.

Really? Well, what are we waiting for? Let's do the cover!

The end!